Italian Writers

Love Letter

Sandro Mayer

Love Letter

Translated from Italian by
Sue Jones

GREMESE

Original title:
Dichiarazione d'amore

Cover:
apostoli & maggi – Rome

Photocomposition:
Graphic Art 6 s.r.l. – Rome
e-mail: dva@uni.net

Printed and bound by:
La Moderna – Rome

GREMESE
1st Edition © 2000
E.G.E. s.r.l. – Rome

ISBN 88-7301-404-6

Dedicated to all those who
have never shared a home
with a creature like you,
a small dog who you will get to
know as you read this book:
to make people realize what
a great love they have missed and
to inspire them to go and look for
it. There are so many
creatures who are just waiting to
give lots of love
in return for nothing at all.

Blessed are you, Oh Lord,
And all your Creatures

Il Cantico delle creature
Saint Francis of Assisi

We kissed when we first met

We first met just over eleven years ago. I came to see you in that shop, as you waited for someone to take you away and give you a home and a little kindness, in return for all that love which you had to give.

You were only supposed to be a present. A present for Isabella's eighteenth birthday. I hadn't seen you yet, and I didn't want you. I would rather have had a bigger dog. Daniela had found you: she was afraid of dogs, all kinds of dogs. But I insisted that this was the perfect present, and she reluctantly agreed. Someone had mentioned that particular shop to her. She liked you because you were so small that it was impossible to be afraid of you. But she was still cautious. She said, "I'm not afraid of her now, because she's so tiny. But she'll still grow up and bark at me, won't she?"

As I said: you were only going to be a present, and I didn't like you. I thought to myself, "It's a silly little poodle." The owner of the shop took me into the back room. You were so small, locked up in a cage. You were only just over four weeks old. He opened the cage, and you rushed out of your prison. Your face was a white ball of fluff, with a dark smudge in the middle for your nose, and two dark specks a bit higher up for eyes. A smaller ball of fluff stuck out from behind: your little tail.

The owner told me that your tail had been longer, but that he had docked it just after you were born, since this was what they did to poodles. I said, "Poor little thing." And then, "Did it hurt her?" He said that it hadn't, but I didn't really believe him.

You were perhaps smaller than the palm of my hand. You ran towards me on your short little legs, which were also white and fluffy, with your tail wagging vigorously: it was your way of letting me know how happy you were to meet me. I bent down to look at you more closely, and placed my hands on the floor. You looked funny as you ran up to me. And you rushed towards me as if you somehow knew that I was the one you had to win over in order to escape from your prison.

I wondered how you knew who I was and why I was there, and told myself that you couldn't possibly know. Later, when I knew you better, I realized that even at that moment when we first met, you already knew, and understood, everything.

But I didn't realize then. I understood so little about you dogs, even though I had one as a child – a white mutt just like you, but with a dark mark which ran right up to his head like a kind of stripe, and then down his neck.

I only had him for three months, and he was taller and longer than you. Much taller and much longer.

I was in Tripoli, one summer. I had gone to Libya to see my dad, who was living over there. I had sailed there with mum and Enrico. Dad was working with grandad in a chemical works on the outskirts of the city. Dad had written to us and described what it was like. And just to make sure we were thoroughly excited and expectant during the three days it took to sail there, he wrote about the dog who guarded the house. I remember how thrilled both Enrico and I were at the prospect of actually seeing that dog.

But my memories of that summer are all muddled now, even though I haven't forgotten the excitement of those first few days, when I played with him, and fought with Enrico because I wanted to feed him too. Enrico was older than I was, though, and yanked him away from me, saying, "You're too little, let me do it." We fought over him as though he were a toy. And now I think about it again, the mongrel seemed happy enough, although I never gave it a moment's thought before. But Enrico and I were too young, and we soon stopped fighting over him, because he was just a toy to us. And just like a child tires of his new toy, so we tired of him. He stayed close, following behind us, but we took no notice of him at all. Only now do I think, "How happy he must have been that he'd found two young masters. And how sad he must have been when we neglected him, how he must have grieved to have lost us so soon. Who knows how often he must have asked himself, 'What did I do wrong to make them abandon me like this?' Because now, I realize that he certainly would have asked himself this.

When we sailed back home three months later, I had already forgotten him. I didn't even say goodbye. We left him guarding the factory, along with an Arab called Mohammed, and with dad, who wrote a week later saying, "Now it's just me and the dog. He's always got his head laid on his paws, and mine is always resting on the table. Neither of us can eat. We're just two sad little dogs." As she read this letter aloud, mum laughed, but I didn't understand. Dad came back about a year later, and the dog was left there all alone.

I didn't give dogs another moment's thought until I started taking our little girl out to the park. While she was playing, she fell over and, as she got up, I saw that she was covered in dog muck. As I cleaned her up using some handkerchiefs dampened in the water fountain, I got angry with dogs, and their owners. Then I decided not to come to the park any more.

Although I wouldn't have actually harmed a dog, I was irritated, and narrow-minded. And so I couldn't understand my friend's sadness when, one lovely sunny day, she came up to me as we sat by the sea, and told me that she had had to take her little spaniel to the vet, because she was ill. She cried and said,

"The vet told me, 'The dog is suffering, and there's nothing we can do for her except put her down.' And so I had her killed. How could I have done it? I try to tell myself that it was all for the best, but now I'm sad because she's not here any more, and also because I had her put down."

She was crying as she told me this, and I felt sorry for her grief, but I didn't really understand it. And I saw how taken aback she was when, trying to cheer her up, I said, "Well, if you miss her so much, why don't you buy another one?" She sobbed out loudly, "You don't understand: you can't replace a loved one just like that."

I didn't want to offend her, so I just looked at her and didn't say any more. But when she'd gone, I said, "It just seems a bit over the top. An animal is just an animal. We must use the word 'love' in its proper context."

I'm not saying that I treated dogs badly, or that I didn't like them. Otherwise I would never have gone into that shop. But it seemed a bit exaggerated for a normal person to cry like that. And maybe – pardon me for saying it – I only went into that shop to buy a toy, just like the mongrel I had as a child. And perhaps I wasn't excited because I was bringing you home, but merely because I'd thought of the best present in the world for Isabella's eighteenth birthday. She had wanted a dog since she was a kid, and we had never given in to her.

These were my thoughts and feelings as you came towards me, but you were about to change all that in an instant. But I didn't know what you were going to do. And I wasn't even aware of how you'd done it. I only realized all this a long time afterwards.

It's incredible: we're unaware of the moment when feelings begin inside us. They just start to gradually, imperceptibly grow. And by the time we realize they're there, the power of love has already taken control of our lives. And we can become completely different to how we were. Even our most ingrained beliefs, which we've held for years, can change.

But this didn't occur to me as I watched you approaching. I looked at you and didn't know what you'd do to me.

As you came up to me in that shop, I asked the owner: "She's so small, will she ever grow?" He replied, "She's a toy poodle, so she'll never get very big. The maximum she'll ever weigh will be five or six kilos."

No, I didn't like you as you came towards me, and you knew it: because later on, when I understood how clever, smart and intelligent you were even then, I realized that you knew, right from that moment, how to read me. But I didn't know then that you understood, and I said aloud, as if you were deaf: "No, I really don't like her at all."

But you understood, blow me if you hadn't understood! In fact, it was then that you made your most surprising move. You stuck out your little tongue, which was just like a tiny pink speck protruding from the white ball of fluff. And you licked my hand: it was your first kiss. And now you're not here any more, my eyes fill with tears, my love, as I remember this. Then you looked right into my eyes, and a shiver went down my back.

But you weren't sure that you'd won me over. And so you kissed me again, playing your best card. You licked my other hand. I was moved and, almost ashamed to be so soft hearted, I blushed. You continued to lick me, giving me a third kiss, and then many others: four, five, ten. Sweetheart, you just couldn't stop yourself. You only did when I placed my hand under your tummy and lifted you up: you were as light as a feather. I brushed your white fur against my face. And this was your moment of triumph: you gave my nose a moist, sweet lick.

Sweetheart, you'd won me over. And you could tell you'd won by the way I held onto you tightly at first, then loosening my grip a little so as not to hurt you.

I told the owner: "I'll take her."

Worn out at last, you proudly settled down against my chest, stretched out in my hand. You had conquered me in less than five minutes. I took you home. And our lives changed from that moment: I became a nicer person with you around. But I wasn't aware of it at first. In fact, there were some difficult times to begin with.

I can remember the first evening. We started off with high ideals. We had rules which had to be followed: you were to sleep alone in the kitchen; you were to pee on the newspaper we put down, while you learnt that you had to do your business outside; we were still going to go out, leaving you at home. In short, we were going to continue just as if you had never come. As if you were a guest. A welcome guest, but no more than a guest all the same.

However, you changed all the rules straight away. That evening, you began to howl so loudly when you were shut in the kitchen that we thought the neighbours would complain. And so, you had the door opened, and you lay down at the foot of Isabella's bed.

And let's not mention the peeing! You went wherever you wanted, and it took lots of time and patience to teach you that you must pee on the newspaper, only on the newspaper.

However, you taught us that you weren't an invader that had come into our lives. And that, even before you started learning the rules, you had certain rights.

It wasn't a question of love yet. But, the morning after that terrible night, we started playing by your rules.

Love came later. I don't know how it grew so much between you and Isabella, or how it became something special between you and Daniela. I was at home so infrequently, and I only saw you during the evenings and weekends. I don't even know how it grew between you and me: all the things I want to recount, and which I'm going to write down, gradually evolved day by day, without my being aware of them.

Perhaps it was only later that I realised, sweetheart, the wonderful things which created the bond between us.

It was only when you'd gone that I began to try and remember every little thing, each and every hour. My thoughts are distinct and ordered: they're all crowding in, but they're not piling up in a heap. I can see everything as if I'm reliving it.

And so I realize that, unwittingly, our moments together remain here where I've written them, day by day, in the ink of life. Here in my heart.

Your name means "pretty" in Greek

It was predictably easy with Isabella: it was love at first sight. She didn't think of you as just a gift. Isabella realized at once that you were you, and that you'd come here to be with her, living one life together.

When you first met, you licked her nose, her eyes and even her mouth. And she cuddled you. And you understood that you were hers and that we, Daniela and myself, were guardians over both of you.

It was Isabella who chose your name: something unique, original, unrivalled. Just as you were unique, original, unrivalled. I suggested: Lulù, Vivì, Mariù. How awful! One day, when you still hadn't got a name, you spent all afternoon lying on Isabella's Greek text book as she studied for her exams. You were already jealous of everything, even this book which held Isabella's attention. You lay on the book so that she would look at you and not at the Greek text. And Isabella just let you lie there. Daniela said, "How can you study like that? Why don't you move her?" She replied, "Her feelings will be hurt, poor little thing." So she had to first of all gently move a paw to one side so that she could read the text. Then she put your paw back in its place, and moved your bottom so that she could read the words underneath. Then she put your bottom back, and looked for the text hidden underneath your muzzle. And it was then, when she saw you sitting looking so pretty on top of that book, and read the Greek words "Καλός, Καλή, Καλόν (Kalós, Kalé, Kalón), which translate as the various Greek cases of the word "pretty", that Isabella pondered on the two words "pretty" and "kalé", and said, one day as we were sitting around the table, "We'll call her Kalé, which means 'pretty' in Greek."

You'd been given a name, and you became our Kalé. You learnt straight away that when we said the sound, "Kalé", that meant you. You understood immediately that you were Kalé, and we introduced you to all our friends by your name: "She's called Kalé, which means 'pretty' in Greek." And whenever we wrote down your name on little notes we left for each other at home, or on some postcard or other, we always wrote your name in Greek: Καλή.

The lambswool coat incident

The hardest nut to crack was Daniela: she was scared of you. The morning following the day of your arrival, after you had spent the night in Isabella's room, you came into our room when she went for a shower. You tried to get up on the bed. You struggled up, panting, with your tongue out. You pulled yourself up by putting your paws up on Daniela's side of the bed. She became edgy, saying: "Oh God, she's climbing up. Please get her away, I'm frightened." I shouted, "Come here." You understood, turned around, and came over to my side of the bed. You barked because you wanted me to lift you up on the bed. I didn't dare.

We got up then, and there was that incident. Daniela opened the shutters, and you started barking so loudly that she became alarmed. You were no bigger than her slipper, but you headed towards her, barking, and she backed up into a corner. The further she retreated, the more you went after her: you seemed to be cornering her. She couldn't stand it any longer, and shouted out to me: "Sandro!" I ran in, dripping wet from the shower. I took one look at the unbelievable sight of you barking as she stood frozen before you as if she were all alone in the jungle facing a lion. She shouted, "She's barking at me. What does she want?" I explained that you were only barking because you were the one who was scared of her. Opening the shutters had made a noise which must have sounded very loud to you.

I said to her, "It's a new sound for her, which is very loud, too loud for her tiny ears. You frightened her, and she's trying to make you stop – look!"

I picked you up, and you stopped barking. You gratefully licked my chin. "You see", I said, "she's quietened down now; hold her, let her know that you didn't mean to scare her."

A miracle occurred: you were passed from my safe arms into her trembling hands. And she touched you, although she was still shaking, and cuddled you for the first time. You went along with it. You reached up towards her face with your nose, but she turned away. You didn't give up, though, and reaching your head up towards her, you licked her wherever you could: you licked her cheeks, her lips and, reaching up further still, even her eyes. She stopped trembling. She realized that she was the stronger of the two, and that you were tiny. She realized that you needed her. And suddenly, she gave in and let you kiss her. The wonderful bond between you was formed right then and there. Of all of us, it's Daniela who feels the loss most of all now that you're no longer with us.

Things were already different the very next morning. I lifted you up onto the bed, and you walked all over us as we slept, wagging your tail, even walking on our heads. And you kissed us. You'd realized right away that you were allowed to do whatever you liked, and that we'd never stop you from doing anything. You did this every morning, right up until the last day that you were with us.

But I hadn't realized quite how much Daniela loved you until that day when, just as we were getting ready to go out, you peed. The time when you didn't pee on the newspaper, like we'd taught you.

All our friends know how much Daniela loves fur coats, whether they're dark or light in color, or whether they're mink or lambswool. She used to say, "I just think of it as survival. If I'm cold, I'd just freeze to death in an overcoat, so I need a fur coat to keep me warm."

She had a wonderful selection of coats, and she kept them all tidily in the wardrobe. She proudly showed them off to friends, took them to a cool storeroom in summer, and went to fetch them again when autumn arrived. One of them was particularly special, as she'd bought it from a well known fashion house. However, this particular pale lambswool coat wasn't actually warm enough. Then she'd had an idea: "I'll have it taken in and shortened, and then I can wear it during the slightly warmer months." And this is what she did.

She brought the coat back home one evening, and proudly showed it to me. It really was very pretty, youthful and charming. She laid it out on the bed. She began to get ready, as we had to go out, and she wanted to wear it straight away. She was sitting in front of the mirror, combing her hair, and the coat was still elegantly draped over the bed behind her. I never understood how or why it happened. Whether it was merely an accident or whether you knew exactly what you were doing, Kalé, because you were so jealous of anything which took our attention away from you. Anyway, the coat had been talked about too much, and she'd tried it on so that I could see how well it suited her, and then tried it on again so that Isabella could see it, and then again in order to reassure herself that it really did look good. Anyway, Kalé, you did have something to be jealous of that evening. The fact of the matter is that I came into the bedroom where she was combing her hair, and where the lovely coat was laid out on the bed, and I saw you.

And, oh boy, what a sight it was. Kalé, you were squatting right in the middle of that highly fashionable lambswool coat, and you were doing the longest pee I have ever seen you do. Right in the middle: as if you had measured the exact distance. Sweetheart, you looked so comical as you looked at me with those knowing eyes, fully aware of what you were doing. I suddenly thought: she'll turn round now, she'll see what's happening and shout. I couldn't even imagine what would happen when she saw you. And so, during that flash, I shouted, "Kalé, what are you doing?"

As I was reaching out to lift you off and put you on the floor, hoping to save whatever it was still possible to salvage, she turned around and told me off, saying, "Leave her be, poor thing." I stood transfixed, as we both watched you finish. Then she said, "You have to leave her alone when she's doing her business. You could scare her if you shout at her."

You finished your business, and moved to one side. But you stayed on the bed and watched Daniela, who mopped up the pee with a cloth, and said, "This mark will never come off, the coat's ruined."

I didn't dare breathe a word, and I couldn't believe that I was seeing the same Daniela. Then she said, "Poor little thing, with all this hustle and bustle, we forgot that it was time to put her on the newspaper so she could do her business. I said, "We must tell her off so that she understands that she mustn't do this again."

Unbelievably, she replied, "What good will telling her off do now? The coat's ruined anyway."

And so it was hung back up in the wardrobe, with your pee stain on it. It's still there, because she never wore it again.

That evening, I realized what a remarkable bond had formed between you, and what great allies you had become, whilst Isabella and myself were out of the house. She wanted to be the one responsible for feeding you, cleaning you, and all your toilet training. She knew everything about you. She inspected the colour of your 'doings', both large and small. She regularly listened to your breathing, and noticed at once if you coughed, or if you had a sore throat. While we were out, a unique, wonderful, incredible relationship developed between you. You belonged only to Isabella, your Isabella. But Daniela was the one who looked after all your needs. And she reported everything to the vet.

When I described the lambswool coat incident to our friends, no-one believed me. It had started off so badly between you, and yet here we were already after only a few months. Kalé, my love, you had won her over.

We begin to communicate

So, Kalé, you had won everyone in the family over, and had become part of our life. There were no longer just the three of us. You were there now, and there were four of us. I never, ever considered for a moment that one day, suddenly, you would leave us.

You learnt to fit in with the family's day, as though you didn't want to cause us any bother. And so, in the morning, once you'd got beyond peeing on newspaper and you wanted to have a sniff outside, you used to come down later, because we went out to work, and you were waiting for Daniela to get ready. At the weekends, since you slept in Isabella's room and she didn't get up very early, you delayed doing your business, sometimes until well after midday.

Daniela took care of feeding you: always boiled chicken and rice, as recommended by the vet. It was all best quality, of course, and your lunch and supper were always served right on time.

At first, we found one of your habits a bit strange. Occasionally, we would find small bits of chicken hidden beneath the cushions on the sofa, or underneath the bedclothes, or even tucked amongst the videos.

We only discovered this because we noticed that you sometimes buried your head amongst the cushions as if checking on something, and then went away again. Once, in order to satisfy our curiosity, we took a look underneath, and discovered the food which you'd hidden away.

"Why does she do that?" Daniela asked me.

I turned towards you, looked you in the eye, and said, "Sweetheart, don't we give you enough to eat? Are you afraid that you'll run out of food, and so you're squirreling away the leftovers?"

You understood what I was saying: your ears were pricked up as if you were trying to hear better. And I saw that you had your head cocked to one side, which you always did when you were really listening to what you were being told.

In an attempt to explain your strange behaviour, I commented: "Perhaps she does it because she was left to go hungry in that shop, and so she's stocking up on food in case those bleak times ever return. Or perhaps it's just an ingrained ancestral thing: the fear of not having enough to eat.

Then I turned back to you and, convinced I had correctly interpreted your behaviour, I stroked you and said, "Sweetheart, you don't have to be afraid of anything ever again now you're with us. This is your home." Seeing you look up at me so sweetly, I really thought I'd managed to reassure you. So I stretched out my hand to retrieve the piece of chicken. But I hadn't convinced you at all. You began to growl, softly at first, and then much louder. You made us understand your terms: we could interpret your actions however we wanted to, but your ways were your ways, and you just wanted to be left in peace. You were growling to make us understand that you weren't happy and, when you weren't happy, we had to back off. And when I didn't back off, but carried on reaching out to take the piece of chicken, you opened your mouth, turned on my hand and seized it. I felt your teeth on my skin, and I began to understand what you were trying to communicate: 'My first growl indicates displeasure and, if you carry on, I'll use my teeth to protect myself, just like you use your hands.'

But I insisted, "Don't do that, sweetheart." Then you let go of my hand, and I thought I had got through to you. But I hadn't done anything of the sort. You stood over the chicken as if to say: 'You're not to touch this.' Then you shouted out your final warning, barking incessantly. And so, when I insisted on reaching for it, you grabbed my hand in your mouth again. This time, I felt your tiny teeth actually clamping down. But you still didn't hurt me. I understood, however, that you were ready to bite me. In short, you knew exactly what you wanted. You were stubborn. I left you with your loot, and walked away, saying, "Bad dog." But you looked defiant, with your head erect, panting with open mouth and tongue hanging out, determined not to give in. You carried on hiding bits of food for another couple of months. And then perhaps you convinced yourself that, in our house, your dish would always be filled at the usual times. And so you stopped.

But that evening proved to be a useful lesson to us all. We'd understood what you meant, the way you expressed yourself, the meaning of your body language. We'd understood what you wanted to say.

I was sorry I'd called you "bad dog", because there are no bad dogs, only people who don't understand them.

From that evening, it became easier to communicate with you. You understood what we were saying, and responded. And we understood your responses.

Only nice words

You soon picked up the words we used which you considered to be the most important ones. The word "food", in particular. Wherever you were, whatever you were doing, whoever you were with, when Daniela shouted from the kitchen: "Food's ready", you dashed straight there, scooting through doors, dodging sofas, weaving past obstacles.

If ever Daniela was delayed, you would come and stand in front of her as she sat on the sofa, talking on the 'phone, and you would look straight at her and begin to bark, quietly at first, and then more forcefully.

You'd only quieten down when you heard her say to whoever she was talking to on the 'phone, "I must go, I've got to get Kalé's food ready", and you would follow her into the kitchen, and lie with your belly flat on the floor and your hind legs stretched out behind, just like a lionskin rug. You used to watch every move she made: you watched her cutting up the chicken into small pieces, you watched her putting the plate into the microwave oven, you watched her take it out and cool the food down before putting it in your blue bowl. Then she'd fill your yellow bowl with water for you, even though you never drank from it.

When you'd finished your meal, you made your own way up to the bathroom, and called out to us. We would come along and find you with your paws in the bidet. We used to turn on the tap and, once the water was coming through nice and clear, you would drink straight from the tap. Right to the end, we used to look on curiously, because we never found out why you liked drinking there so much. "Maybe she prefers running water", we wondered. "Perhaps it tastes fresher like that." It's the only thing we never understood about you, and which you were never able to explain to us.

But let's carry on with your vocabulary. The other word you liked to hear was 'bags'. You learnt what this meant straight away.

You were still tiny then, and Isabella liked to go to the seaside every Friday evening. I couldn't go, but I made sure I saw you off at the station. When I left the house in the morning, I used to say, "I'll see you tonight on the train, because you're going to the seaside." I used to tell you this in a cheerful tone of voice, and you understood that something nice was going to happen.

A bit later on, Daniela would pack the bags: she'd get them down from the wardrobe, pack them and then leave them in the corner of the room. You used to go over and sniff at them every now and again, because you could smell your things inside. Then, towards the end of the day, a great hustle and bustle. 'Call the taxi', 'Get the bags', 'Where's Kalé's litte coat?' And then you, Isabella and Daniela used to arrive at the station, where I would be waiting for you all. We'd have to run for the train, because we were always late. I used to wave you off from the platform as you boarded the train. I used to meet you at the station again the next day, or sometimes wait for you at home. It was the same routine, every Friday. And so you learnt the meaning of the words 'bags', 'seaside', 'train', 'let's run', 'hurry', 'late'.

You liked going to the seaside because we let you off the lead to run about on the beach, and you just loved the open space, where you couldn't hear any traffic. And so the words associated with our Friday routine stuck in your little mind. When I got up in the morning, I only had to say, "Off to the seaside this evening" and, incredibly, you would go over to the wardrobe where the bags were kept and scratch at the door to try and make it open so you could get them out.

You were so overjoyed when Daniela packed the bags that you just stood watching her. You would occasionally go over to the corner where they were put just to make sure they were still there, and that our plans hadn't changed: we really were going to the beach.

Then you learnt the words "let's go" and "let's go out". These were your favourites. When you got bored with wherever we had brought you, you just longed to hear “let’s go!” It might have seemed that you were sleeping under the table at our friend’s house, or in the restaurant, and that you were taking no notice whatsoever of what was going on around you or with what we were involved in. However, as you lay stretched out on the floor, even if you had your head down, you were still following everything, because as soon as you heard us say “let’s go”, you would jump up, wagging your tail, and head for the door. You had learnt by noticing that the words “let’s go” were always followed by our getting up and heading towards the door.

You liked “Let’s go out” even more. Daniela had taught you what it meant, because it was she who took you out the most while we were out at work. And this is how you learnt what it meant. You used to watch her with sad eyes, in the bathroom as she got dressed and put perfume on, afraid that she was going to leave you all alone in the house. So she used to tell you, “Don’t be sad, we’re going out.” You learnt to recognize what was coming next. She would put your lead on, open the door, and call the lift. And when she realized that you understood what she meant, Daniela used to say “Let’s go out” even before she started getting ready, just so you wouldn’t be sad even for a moment. She used to say it in a cheerful tone of voice, which you learnt to associate with nice things.

And so, day by day, linking the words you heard us say, and with our actions, you learnt our vocabulary. It was wonderful, because we could talk to you. We spoke, and you reacted. We would say "Let's go", and you would get up to go. We would say "Let's go out", and you headed for the door. "Let's get a taxi", and you would head for those white cars at San Babila Square, driven by those men whom you didn't know, but whom you liked because they gave you a ride.

"Isabella's coming", and you went to the front door so you could go and wait by the lift.

And, incredibly, you even learnt our commands. "We're going to be in the car a long time, you'd better go and pee", and you immediately sniffed at the ground and squatted to do your business. "Stop bothering me, I want to sleep", and you would very gently lie down very quietly next to us.

And then you learnt how to ask for things, and to answer our questions, and we began to enjoy your company even more as we were able to hold conversations with you. "Do you want a drink?", to which you answered "Yes" with a yap, and headed for the bathroom as one of us came with you to turn on the bidet tap. Or else you made your own way to the bathroom, and called us from there. Quietly at first. You used to make a low sound in your throat, almost as if you were growling continuously. You'd only stop when you heard one of us coming to turn on the tap. If we didn't come straight away because we were on the 'phone, or the detective on the TV was just about to find out who the murderer was, you called a little louder. You gave a short bark, and then waited a moment before giving another, then a third, and then a fourth short, sharp bark. And if we still didn't come because the police hadn't arrested the murderer yet, you used to stand indignantly in the doorway and look at us from afar, barking loudly, incessantly, wagging your tail and continually looking towards the bathroom as if to say, "Don't you realize that I'm thirsty and I'm tired of waiting around?" And then one of us had to get up then and there, because otherwise you would never have stopped barking and, if it was late, you would have woken all the neighbours.

If we went for a cup of coffee at a café, you used to ask for some water. As soon as you saw a waiter taking a bottle to a table, or if you saw a waiter putting a glass on the counter, you used to look at us, bark, and then look at the glass. We understood what you wanted, and we would ask the waiter, "Could you pour a little water into a paper cup, please?" They realized it was for you, and often asked, "Do you want a bowl?" "No, thank you, a paper cup will be fine." We used to prefer that you had a paper cup, because we were always concerned that the dish might be dirty. I would kneel down and hold the cup tilted slightly towards you so that you could drink, as the cup was a bit narrow for you to easily reach right to the bottom. And everyone would watch us.

It was slightly different at the restaurant. We would always order still mineral water: *we* liked carbonated water, but you didn't. The green bottle would be there on the table. You didn't always ask for some, but you would sometimes grumble away under the table. Not loudly, as you did at home, but just so we could hear you. We didn't want anyone to see us, so we used to pour a little water into the ashtray, and sneak it down to you hidden behind a napkin, so that you could drink unseen beneath the table.

At home, you always used to lie down beside me as we ate, because rather than a chair, I used to sit on a bench, which was long enough for both of us. You would lie with your head resting on the cushion. You didn't make any fuss, because Daniela always used to feed you first. Occasionally, however, when you wanted some attention, or you still felt a bit hungry, you'd beg for food. First, you'd paw at my arm, and I used to look down at you. I knew what you wanted, but I'd say, "What do you want?" You'd reply with a long, throaty sound. I used to ask, "Do you want a bit of bread?", and you'd answer 'Yes' with another long sound. I'd give you a piece of bread, and you'd take it between your teeth and put it on the cushion. You'd hold it down with your paw and begin to gnaw at it. We gave you special bread: a few days' old, and a bit hard, because the vet said that it was good for your digestion.

And so, these were our conversations. These were

our meals. This is how we became friends. We notice the silence at the table now. We talk, the television is on, the 'phone rings. But there's still a silence, my love. When you were here, it often felt as though you weren't around, because you were in another room or asleep on the sofa. Now that you're no longer here, we seem to see you everywhere: on the bench, at the restaurant with us, at the café, in front of the TV in the lounge. We think we hear you barking. But we're surrounded by silence. You weighed just five kilos, you weren't even half a meter long, and were a little longer than the palm of my hand. So small, but you managed to fill the house.

More than just a gift

You hadn't been with us very long, and I began to wonder why I loved you so much. I asked myself this because it just seemed amazing that I had this desire within me to protect you, to give you things, to make you happy, and to keep you safe. I often thought, "Is she happy with us? Would she have been better off with someone else?" I wondered, and felt silly.

I took you for walks in my spare time. You even came with me on Saturday and Sunday mornings to the auctions which they held in the antique showrooms, knowing that they would stop us at the door and say, "You must hold onto the dog." So I used to pick you up and cuddle you against me as I meandered around looking at furniture and antique lampstands.

You enjoyed being carried around. You used to feel safe in my arms, and you gazed proudly at those who were at the same eye level. I knew how proud you were, because you would sit up attentively, looking at everything and everyone. You used to turn your head this way and that, gazing curiously at everything I stopped to look at. I used to watch you and say,

"Kalé, are you trying to figure out why I like this so much?" When I spoke to you, you would look up towards me and lick my face. And so, when we were out together, I began to understand how much you enjoyed being carried around, and how much you enjoyed being involved in everything I was doing or looking at, as I talked to you.

You weren't heavy, but I would get tired after a while and put you down again. But you were like a spoilt child, and you would put your paws on my shins and reach up towards me. You looked so sweet. You were so tiny that you only came up to my knees. Then you would wag your tail: it was your way of asking. I knew what you wanted, and I used to say: "Do you want me to pick you up again?"

Of course, "pick you up" was another phrase which you came to know, and you were overjoyed when you heard it. And so I would pick you up again, saying: "I'm only going to carry you for a little while, because I'm tired. After all, I'm getting old, you know." And you would lick my face, trying to reach my mouth, like you always did when you were really happy: it was your way of showing how much you loved someone. I must confess, I enjoyed carrying you, too, because I could feel your warm belly, your soft fur, and the slow rhythm of your breathing.

And yet, I wondered *why* I enjoyed it. And then, as I cuddled you, I would tell myself, "I love you because you're Isabella's, and I love you because she loves you. I'm doing all this because I know Isabella would be pleased." I always got the impression that you didn't like this conversation, because it was one of the few times you didn't kiss me, but just lay still in my arms. Was this just an impression, or did you really understand? Was it just imagination, or did you actually understand when I told Isabella all this? She asked me, "You love Kalé, don't you?" I replied, "Of course I do, because I love you." You suddenly walked off, and I had the feeling that you went because you didn't want to hear any more. And so you didn't hear Isabella angrily saying: "You should love her just for herself, not because you love me."

But I found it hard to believe that I actually just loved *you* so much. Such strong feelings must, of course, be due to my love for Isabella.

Later on, however, I became convinced that I loved you purely for yourself. So I told Isabella: "Now I love her just because she's Kalé. It could have been that from the start, but I didn't realize, or didn't like to admit it."

And, incredibly, you came up to me and lovingly, knowingly, licked my face.

Now you're not here any more, the memories overlap and run into each other when I think about you and the times we had together, and I lose track. I haven't actually mentioned *how* I came to know that I loved you purely for yourself, that it was a bond just between the two of us, you and I, completely different to the loving relationship you had with Isabella, and to the intimacy which existed between Daniela and yourself.

I made you feel stronger, safer. Daniela commented: "When we're out walking, she never asks me to pick her up. She asks you to pick her up because she feels safe in your strong arms. You make her feel calm. She understands that you're a man, and she feels protected." I often wondered if I'd have loved you quite as much if you'd been a male dog. I thought that I probably wouldn't have. The fact that you were female made me feel that our relationship was closer, that you held fragile kind of respect towards me, so that I would protect you.

And so it was that I discovered I loved you, and needed you. It was a foul day, Isabella was out, and I picked a fight with Daniela over something and nothing. We argued, and shouted at each other. In relationships, this happens sometimes, but unfortunately for you, on this occasion, you has to listen to us. For you, this was something unheard of. I later realized that you couldn't get your head around the fact that, suddenly, two people who loved each other could lose all respect, even if it was only temporarily. So when you heard all the shouting, you went and hid under the bed, as if to take shelter. Poor little thing, I guess if the front door had been open that day, you would have run far, far away, and who knows if you'd ever have come back. So there you were beneath the bed, and I only realized afterwards how much you were shaking. I sat down on the sofa as the argument continued. From the bedroom, you could hear my footsteps going into the study, and you heard me sitting down.

I hadn't even had time to lean back on the sofa when you ran up to me faster than I've ever seen you run before. You leapt up onto my lap, with your ears down and a terrified expression on your face. And you were trembling, shaking all over! I placed my hand on your chest and felt your heart hammering. It seemed as though your legs, your head, your back were almost going to explode. I was scared that something had happened to you. I stopped speaking, and put an end to our heated discussion. I began gently stroking you. Daniela quietened down too. But you were still trembling more and more violently. I held you close to me, kissed you on top of your head, and murmured gently to you. At that moment, I was afraid that I'd never be able to calm you down. But when you sensed that peace was returning, your trembling subsided. I carried on kissing you. You eventually raised your head, reached up towards me and licked my face. And you showed me how grateful you were that I'd swallowed my anger.

Perhaps you were frightened because you didn't know who was being shouted at, and you were afraid that we were angry with *you*. Maybe this is why you hid under the bed, and then came running up to me for forgiveness. Or perhaps you were afraid that our peaceful home had been permanently disrupted. You used to worry about yourself, about us, about the whole family. You reminded us what a great blessing it is to have peace and quiet.

I realized at that moment that you weren't just a gift any more, but the fourth member of our family. You had your own needs, and we had to respect your rights. You hadn't asked to be brought here. We'd come looking for you, as if searching for a child, a lifelong companion, a friend. And when one goes looking for, and finds, something he needs, he must then respect it, even if it's only a tiny creature like you. You were no longer just a gift, or just a belonging, nor had you ever been. But now I understood that you were an individual in your own right.

And that's how I thought of you from that day onward.

Sometime later, Isabella asked me again: "Do you still love her only because you love me?" I spoke from my heart. "I love her because she's Kalé. I've loved her for some time."

And I was being completely honest.

Our wonderful times at Christmas

Even Christmas was a happier time with you there. We always used to have a party at Christmas time. We all got together at grandma's house – our aunts and uncles, all the cousins, and us. The Christmas tree would be covered in gifts, with so many brightly coloured parcels all on the floor in a heap which was almost as high as the tree itself. I told grandma that you'd be coming along too this year, and that we'd only had you a little over a month.

"For goodness' sake, don't you bring her along," grandma commanded. She'll pee all over the carpet." We told her that we couldn't come either unless we brought you, because you were too small to leave all alone in the house until so late in the evening.

We lied: "We don't trust her enough yet to leave her all alone". To be truthful, we didn't want to leave you out of such a lovely family occasion. We managed to convince her that, if you really had to do your business, you would go on some newspaper. However, although we did manage to persuade her, she was still reluctant to let you into the house.

You sat quietly on my lap throughout the meal.

You hid your head under my napkin as though you didn't want anyone to see you: you sensed that there was hostility towards you. Every now and again, you could hear grandma commenting: "If she does a pee on my carpet, you'll have to take her straight home." You couldn't understand what she was saying, of course, because it was the first time you'd seen this woman, who must have seemed very bad-tempered to you. But you didn't like her tone of voice, and you sat very quietly on my lap. You knew that, whatever happened, I would protect you. After we'd eaten, we gathered around the Christmas tree to unwrap all the presents. There was a name tag on each parcel, and we all hunted excitedly for our gifts. You joined in the scrimmage as well, and dived in amongst the parcels. You were so tiny that all those boxes wrapped in brightly coloured paper caused you to tumble upside down. We could see a little white bottom, but the rest was hidden by parcels. You tail was wagging vigorously. I didn't understand what you were up to, but then you re-emerged, gripping a parcel in your teeth. I said: "Put it down." "Don't break it, it's not yours." But you gave me a challenging stare, and I could tell you were annoyed because your tail stopped wagging. You'd decided that you were going to keep hold of your prize.

Daniela came back into the room with grandma then, from the kitchen where they'd taken the dirty dishes. She saw you, and exclaimed: "That's unbelievable! How did you find it? You're so clever, Kalé." And as everyone looked round to see what Kalé had done that was so clever, Daniela explained: "I wrapped a little present for her, too, but how did she manage to find it?" We hadn't realized until then how powerful your sense of smell was. Your nose had led you to your present, and now you wanted to tear off the paper. You held it down with your paws, and ripped off the wrapping with your teeth, making the paper go all soggy with your wet tongue. We watched, fascinated, as you revealed the gift which your nose had sought out: a small chewing ring – just one of the many little presents they sold specifically for little dogs like you. You liked the smell of it, and started gnawing on the tough ring straight away.

You'd managed to win grandma over, as she watched you in admiration, chewing on the ring for hours on end. She said, "Isn't she good, she's no bother at all." But it was later that you really bowled her over. I don't know whether it was because you didn't want to make her cross, or because the chewing ring had kept you occupied all evening, but you still hadn't gone for a pee even as we were getting up to leave. Grandma thought that this was the best thing ever, and the fact that her carpets had survived without any lasting stains, made her Christmas just perfect.

You became the best of friends as time went on, and she welcomed you with open arms whenever we went to visit. You were warmly welcomed every Christmas after that.

It had started off so badly between the two of you, all because of that dreaded pee which never happened, but when I had to tell her you weren't with us any longer, she couldn't sleep. Her legs trembled, and she wept as she remembered how well trained you were. "She came to the house so many times, and she never once made a mess." That was her way of showing how much she loved you.

Kalé, everyone has different memories about you. You understood each of us, and you pleased and delighted all of us, as if you really knew and understood our characters, the individual personality of each one of us. You let grandma have the very thing that was closest to her heart: the almost obsessive cleanliness of her home. And once, when we got caught in a downpour on the way to visit her, and you had wet paws, you stopped outside the front door and wouldn't go in when she opened it. You heard her saying, "Dear me, how wet you all are", and waited until I dried you off before you went in.

An evening of Shakespeare at the theater

As time went by, you gradually won over all our friends. We only occasionally left you alone in the house, when you definitely weren't allowed wherever we were going: the cinema, or the casino. But if a restaurant said that dogs weren't allowed, then we just didn't go there.

When we went to the cinema, Daniela would tell you: "We really can't take you with us tonight, but we'll be back in a couple of hours." You always understood, and miserably crawled under the bed, because you just couldn't bear to see her getting ready to go out without you.

Daniela was always in a worse state than you when she couldn't take you with her. She used to talk to you as she put on her make-up in front of the mirror: "Come on, Kalé, please don't be like that just because I'm going to the cinema for a change. Come out and talk to me."

You wouldn't budge, however. You refused to be consoled, and stayed in your hiding place. But you never used to bear a grudge. It would always be as wonderful to see you so overjoyed when we returned, as it had been horrible to see you so upset when we went out.

When you saw us coming back, you immediately forgot all the anguish we'd caused you. As the key turned in the lock, we could hear you sniffing under the door: you wanted to make sure it was really us. Then we used to hear you whining and scratching at the door with your paw: you were trying to get it open before I even managed to turn the key, to break it down, to pull down that barrier which stood between us. And then, there we were: you jumped up at us, licking us, wagging your tail to let us know how pleased you were to see us. You shared your attentions out equally between us, not a second too long with her, not a second too short with me. We thought that you were probably afraid of offending one of us by showing the other more affection. But you loved all three of us in your own way. And so, if Isabella came out with us, you would jump up at her first of all, then at Daniela, and then you used to come and seek me out, as I would always stand back a little, to one side, in the belief that you were less bothered about me than the other two. But you would come and find me, and give me the same amount of attention and licks as you had given them.

Then you used to run to the room where all your toys were kept. You'd grab hold of the first one you came to: a chewing ring, a rag doll, a fake bone which smelled nice. And you'd bring it to us, but you'd never give it to us. You used to jump up on the sofa, holding on to it tightly in your mouth, and proudly show it to us. I never understood why you used to run and fetch a toy every time someone came to the house. We often wondered, but this was one puzzle which was never resolved.

And so, our friends. You were always very affectionate towards them, and you soon won them over. They came to love you, and to understand your ways, as they saw you were always with us. You didn't cause a nuisance, and they would always comment: "Isn't she good! She's so quiet."

You used to sit under the table when we were at a restaurant, and you sat on our laps when we went round to someone's house for a meal. We often took you along to the beach, and you'd lie down beneath our sun loungers, in the shade.

There was only one thing which our friends were not allowed to do. It only took one occasion to make us understand this: and it was such an uproarious event that the voices still echo in my mind. On one of the first occasions that we took you into a restaurant, a friend of ours ordered: "Steak, well done, please."

Daniela and I both turned sharply and glared at him. "What did I do?" he asked in a small, quiet voice.

"How can you order steak with Kalé here?"

You loved steak best of all, but we couldn't ever let you have any, because it made you ill.

We insisted: "It'll be completely unbearable for her,

and she'll start making a fuss." Then I said, in a tone of voice which may have come across as sarcastic, but wasn't meant as such: "Use a bit of common sense, for goodness' sake. When we've got Kalé with us, surely you could order something other than meat for a change?"

Everyone burst out laughing, and the event was reported back to other friends as a bit of a laugh. "When you take Kalé out for a meal, don't dare order meat, because you'll get told off!"

It was all a big joke to them. But, actually, when it was just us at the restaurant – myself, Daniela and you – we never ordered meat, or anything which would make your mouth water, but which you weren't allowed to have.

This was also an indication of our respect, of our love for you. And so our friends had to learn how to socialize with us when you were there as well. And when, occasionally, we met up without bringing you along, they used to enquire, even before saying hello: "Where's Kalé?"

And to think we even managed to take you along with us to the theater on occasions. Our friend Enrico owned an open air theater at the seaside, which played host to well known theater companies every summer. We often went along, and we didn't want to have to leave you at home all the time. And so we used to arrive, carrying you, and Enrico would say with a big smile: "You've brought Kalé", and he would gently stroke you, because he really liked you. We said, "Yes, but only one of us can go into the theater, and the other will stay outside with Kalé." We already knew what Enrico would say: "No, I wouldn't hear of it. You must take her in – just stay at the back, and if she makes a noise, you can come straight out again." The theatre was always packed, and we used to sit near the back wall, so that no-one would see you. You used to sit in our arms, with your head up, listening to the actors' dialogue. You watched everything. But did you ever make a fuss, or bark? You watched plays by Shakespeare, Goldoni, and Molière. You were introduced to famous actors and actresses whom we met backstage after the show, and they all had a kind word for you: "Aren't you sweet! Did you see the show? Did you enjoy it?" You never made a fuss, and you never became impatient, even if it was particularly long show. You enjoyed being in that theater, in that square where there was always a fresh, gentle evening breeze. You remained quiet, perhaps understanding that you weren't really allowed to be there, because you never saw or smelt any other dogs there.

You also understood, by the absence of certain familiar smells, that you were in a special place and, at the end, you would always wag your tail against Enrico's legs and wait for him to stroke you.

You liked Enrico, too. Maybe because he let you go into the theater.

You slept beside me

You enjoyed being with us all the time, but didn't particularly enjoy being with other dogs. As time went by, we noticed that when we were out walking and you saw another dog coming, you would pull away on the lead in order to avoid meeting it. And when they came up and sniffed at you...! You hardly ever allowed it and, on the few occasions when you did, it was only to let the friend you'd bumped into sniff at you very briefly. Then off you'd go, and if the other dog followed too, you'd turn around, annoyed, and bark so loudly, baring your teeth, that it would be terrified, however large or small, and run away.

Although you were so tiny, they were all scared of you. The only thing you were afraid of was Alsatians. You sensed by smell when an Alsatian was in the vicinity, even from afar. It would be around the corner, but you'd be aware that it was there, and you used to bark loudly to let us know that you wanted to go a different way. You always barked when you were scared, even when a stranger – a plumber, an electrician or a furniture delivery man – came to the door. You were as fierce and loud towards other creatures and strangers as you were placid and quiet with us.

Other people who studied your behaviour always took delight in telling me that it was our fault that you weren't good at socializing with other dogs. Dogs are just like children: you must not smother them with affection, or lavish too much attention on them. Dogs also need space and freedom in which to grow up. But because we always kept you beside us on a leash, this had made you insecure around others, and, in particular, we'd caused you to stop wanting to be with other dogs. You preferred to be with our friends: they spoiled you and made you feel safe. Who knows whether you were really happy living just with us, and not with other animals of your own kind? Who knows whether you'd have had a much better life if you'd been brought up in a household where you had a bit more freedom. These are the thoughts and concerns of someone who loves another. These are the questions which go through one's mind only later, when a loved one has gone.

But it was impossible to love you in any other way. Isabella was always more aware of your rights, and said to us: "Leave her be, leave her on her own in the house a bit more, she's got to find her own way, it's not good to be living like that."

Isabella's way of loving you was definitely more sensible. She loved you very much, but she knew how to be rational about it too. I don't know much about the bond which existed between you, because when Isabella was there, you were never with me. She would pick you up and carry you to her flat which is next to ours. She closed the door behind you both, and there you would live out your lives together. We only looked after you when she wasn't at home.

She expressed her love for you differently to us, and was sometimes much more strict with you. It affected you profoundly, because as soon as you saw her, you would leave us and scoot off to her place. There was a wonderful bond between you: so gentle, so unique. You even licked her differently. You used to lick her nose and cheeks, and she would hug you. You would look at us watching you as if trying to tell us that these were special kisses, just for her.

There were no rules when you were with me, however. I just let you do whatever you liked. When you stayed with us overnight, you used to sleep stretched out over my stomach, as if you were glued there. Sometimes, I would wake up during the night and I would see that, without waking me, you had snuggled up by my face. You had laid your head on the pillow, and were stretched out on your side, just as I was. I would look at you with sleepy eyes and just let you be. I enjoyed knowing you were so close by. I would stroke you as you lay there, and then go back to sleep.

I even took you to the office

You even came along to work with me. You were only a little over six months' old when I first took you. I don't remember why, but Isabella and Daniela were away. You usually went with them, but they couldn't take you on that particular day. You were left completely in my care for the first time: I had to feed you, make sure you did your business, and keep you company. But you were a little nervous at being left alone with me.

You watched me dejectedly as I cut up your chicken in the morning. Suddenly, you started barking. I realized I'd done something wrong, but I didn't know what it was. I said: "I know something's not quite right, but don't shout. Try and explain." The more I talked, the more you barked. So I decided to retrace my steps and do everything again. I put the chicken back in the fridge. You looked at me strangely, as if to say: "What are you doing now?" Then I opened the fridge door again, took the chicken out, and started cutting it up once again. I tipped it off the plate and into your bowl. And then you started barking again. So I realized that I'd gone wrong somewhere between cutting up the chicken and putting it into your bowl. I repeated out aloud what I'd done, feeling a bit silly, with you still barking and making a din. Then I yelled: "I know what it is!", thumping the table in triumph. "I have to wash your bowl: that's it, isn't it?" So I turned around, tipped the chicken back onto the plate, and washed your bowl. As if by magic, you stopped barking. Then I dried the bowl, put the chicken in it, which then went into the microwave and finally into your tummy. You'd made me understand.

This was how our day together began. I didn't really know what to do with you, as I couldn't leave you on your own all day. So I took you to work with me. We arrived quite early, and you trembled in my arms as we walked through the underground car park where we'd left the car. It was all new and strange to you, and you didn't feel very safe.

We went up to my office, and you slowly got to know your way around, and to recognize the various people. I introduced you to whoever came into my office, and explained what you were doing there. And you could tell from the tone of my voice that I was a little uncomfortable with the situation, and you started to feel awkward too, as if you realized that you shouldn't be there. You were lying on a chair that I'd pulled up next to mine, and you lay quite still as people came and stroked you.

Then Grazia came in, and brought some ham cut

up into little pieces on a paper plate for you. I'd asked her if she would be able to do this for you at lunch time, so she'd got it from the canteen. You took an immediate liking to this blond lady, because she had made a fuss of you. But it was Osvaldo with whom you formed an immediate, special bond. You already knew him, because we often went out together on Saturday morning. It was a huge surprise for you to discover him here, in my office. It must have been a wonderful discovery, because you jumped off the chair and went straight up to him, wagging your tail. Everything felt a bit less strange then, and you dared to get down from the chair and sniff all round the office. But you didn't make any mess. Osvaldo was surprised to see you, too. He said: "Kalé, what are you doing here?", kneeling down so that he could stroke you. And you gave him lots of kisses. You immediately recognized Osvaldo as a safe haven. His office was right next to mine, and there was an adjoining door between the two rooms that we left open all that day. And so, when I had to leave my office, you weren't all alone. "I'm just popping out for a moment", I said, "I'll be back soon." And when I returned, I found you sitting on Osvaldo's lap. He told me: "She came into my office as soon as you went out. She pawed at me and jumped up. She's been there all the time." Osvaldo was seated at his desk, working, and you were just lying on his knees. Left alone in that strange place, you'd thrown yourself into the arms of the only person you recognized there.

You sensed that he liked you. And as you lay on his lap, he could see how lovely you were. He stroked you, and, he told me, you responded with kisses. He'd never known anything like it. After he'd had you sitting on his knee, however, he'd taken a liking to dogs and, a few months later, he too bought a little dog: Ruud, a sheepdog puppy.

When it was time to go home that evening, there was no-one left in the office. You were fed up with staying in one place. I was still there with you in the office as Osvaldo went over to the lift at the end of the corridor. He waited for us. You saw him. The corridor between us was at least fifty metres long. And you hurled yourself along at top speed to reach him.

You needed to stretch your legs. I stayed where I was and, when you reached him, I called: "Come on Kalé, come here. Come on, Kalé." And you came back the other way. You realized that you were even allowed to play in this place which had seemed so strict during the day, and you ran back barking. You rushed along so fast that your ears blew back and flapped behind you. You looked like a little rabbit.

"Come on, Kalé", shouted Osvaldo from the other end, and you tirelessly ran up and down the corridor.

The ham, the running, the memory of that day – it all made a big impression on you.

And so, when I had to take you to the office with

me again, I used to tell you: "We're going to the office today", and you weren't afraid any more. You were happy to come along.

You would wait for Osvaldo to arrive. And when I had to leave my office, you would always run over to Osvaldo. You would wag your tail when Grazia brought you some ham. But you used to stay on the chair when other people came into my office, because you understood that you mustn't cause a disturbance. And you never once disturbed me, or distracted me from my work for even a moment, or caused me to miss a meeting.

I didn't take you to work more than six or seven times during the ten years. But even my colleagues there remember you. When he's talking about you, Osvaldo says: "She felt so soft, sitting on my lap", and I see a sadness in his eyes. "It's amazing: she used to jump right into my arms as soon as you left your office. My dog Rudd goes off and does his own thing, but she always wanted to be near someone."

When I leave the office in the evening and I see Osvaldo waiting at the end of the corridor while I close and lock my door, I can hear the echo of your barking. Your presence is always there along that corridor. And I see you running. Every evening.

Fate was about to take an interest in our happiness

And so, the day came when we began to lose you. You didn't go straight away, but it was then, on that day, that our lives changed. You didn't notice anything at all. Perhaps you just wondered why a gloom had descended over that particular day's holiday.

Right up until that day, we never thought that anything could ever be different, or that you would leave us, that fate would come along and take an interest in our happiness and decide to take you away from us.

It was the end of summer. I flew to Nizza, while you and Daniela, having already been on vacation, came directly from Liguria to meet me at the airport. Isabella was elsewhere. I distinctly remember that it was Saturday. Eleven o' clock in the morning, or just after. When you saw me coming out of the exit tunnel, you pulled hard on the lead, wanting Daniela to let you loose. She did so, and you ran right up to me, weaving amongst the passengers who were in front of me, or even going right between their legs, because you were small enough to fit through. Your happy tail was wagging excitedly. Your mouth was open and your hot, dry tongue was hanging out. You were so lovely that everyone turned to look at you. Whenever I was due to arrive, Daniela would say to you: "Come on, let's make ourselves beautiful, and then we'll go to the airport because Sandro's arriving. Then some friends are coming round tonight, and we're going out. You can't possibly go to the restaurant looking like that, what would people think?" And so you allowed her to brush you, and your fur would become soft and shiny. Then she'd tidy your muzzle, and clean your paws, ears, nose, and even your bottom, with a damp cloth. Then she'd trim your coat a little with a large pair of scissors. She used to cut off the straggly bits, because they bothered you. But she never had you clipped. You had a wonderful coat, and Isabella didn't want it cut short. She just tidied it up a bit with the scissors. But she always made sure that she left the fur on your muzzle thick and fluffy, just like the fur on your back and feet. You didn't really like it when she was tidying you up, but you allowed her to do it, because you knew that, after you'd endured this torment, I would soon be there, and then friends would arrive and we would go out for the evening, all of which you enjoyed. You enjoyed socializing, and you loved being surrounded by happy people. And our friends knew that, when they came out with us, you would be coming along too, because you came with us everywhere, and we would just have to avoid any place which didn't allow dogs.

And so you came running up to me on that Saturday, and I knelt down to cuddle you and let you lick me, and everyone looked at us. But I wasn't embarrassed, and I didn't feel silly for loving you so much, or for being loved by you. In fact, as you were licking me, I thought that everyone in the airport was probably jealous.

We caught a taxi, and you fidgeted on my lap because you wanted to move around, to jump up and lick my face. But I made sure you never made a fuss when we were in a taxi, because you were afraid of dirtying the seats, and that the driver would tell us off, as had happened many times before when my attention wandered. I watched you, stroked you, and said: "Aren't you lovely." I turned to Daniela: "Did you give her a bath? She's lovely and clean." "No, I just brushed her a bit. She was a bit messy, and I couldn't let her come in that state. She'd just jump up and people would get annoyed if she wasn't nice and clean." You always smelled nice, because your fur was always fragrant. I said: "What's she talking about, Kalé? You're always lovely", and I buried my face into your fur and breathed in. But Daniela refused to take part in the little games that you and I loved playing together. She stared out of the window, lost in thought.

"What's wrong?" I asked her. "What's the matter?"

She replied: "Nothing, honestly", but her voice couldn't disguise that fact that, deep down, she was worried about something. She wanted to talk, but didn't dare in case she spoiled my holiday.

I asked her again: "Come on, what's happened? Tell me." But I honestly never thought that her reply would have been the start. The start of our final goodbye, Kalé.

She said: "I'm worried because, while I was brushing Kalé today, I felt something on her belly, near one of her teats."

"What sort of thing?" I asked, trying to sound calm and composed, but feeling my heart leap into my mouth. As I felt amongst the fur on your belly, she said: "It can't be anything serious, of course, because she's so lively, and looks so well." I told her: "Let's not make a mountain out of a molehill just yet." Then, as if to reassure her, I jokingly said: "Come on, show me this thing which you felt", trying desperately all the while to calm the panic rising inside me.

The taxi was going along Promenade des Anglais, and I could see the holidaymakers wilting beneath the blazing sunshine, happy to be on vacation. Everything around was beautiful: the little villages in the hills, the vivid blue sea, the crowded restaurants.

I couldn't have wished for better surroundings in which to begin my vacation, but there I was, sitting in a taxi, feeling around for something with my fingertips as she guided my hand. I didn't know what is was. But I felt around until I found it. It was a tiny lump. So small that I thought it might be one of your teats at first. Actually, it was the first sign of the disease which would take you away from us. But how could I ever have known that fate would find us there in that taxi as we drove along the streets of that wonderful place? That fate would come along and ask us to pay the bill for the ten wonderful years we'd been given? You'd actually celebrated your tenth birthday only the previous day, and Daniela, as she always did, had treated you to some meat.

And now fate had come along and wanted us to pay up.

Trying to reassure both Daniela and myself, I said: "It'll just be a bit of an inflammation, that's all. We'll take her to the vet when we get back to Milan."

She agreed, not in the least reassured.

I remembered that we always used to pass a veterinary surgery when we went out together to the antique shops. It was a small animal hospital which always seemed to be open. I used to notice it as we walked by, but I never thought for a moment that we would need to go there, because one always believes that these things only happen to other people. But this time, sweetheart, it had happened to us. To you.

I said: "We can't possibly wait until we return to Milan. Let's go and see someone here. I know where there's a place, close to where all the antique shops are."

She said: "I don't feel right going to see someone here. I don't really know any of them."

But she sounded uncertain, and only wanted to delay the moment of truth. I just didn't want to believe that the truth could possibly be that which, in fact, we actually knew all along, and insisted: "Come on, you'll see that it's nothing serious, and it'll put our minds at rest." And I instructed the taxi driver to take us there.

We got to the veterinary surgery, and you didn't want to go in, because you could smell that we'd arrived somewhere similar to the vet's we used to take you to see in Milan, and that a strange doctor would come and make you lie you down on the couch, touch you, examine you. As he felt around the swelling, the expression on his face seemed to indicate that things weren't quite right. He told us: "We'd have to take an X-ray to be absolutely sure." We asked him to do so, and he did. He spoke in a normal tone of voice. Every word was like a blow to our hearts, as he calmly, concisely explained the problem. As if he didn't really care. You were our Kalé: he didn't know you and, as we'd just dropped by, he didn't know us well enough either to care about our feelings.

And so he stated in a brisk, matter of fact way: "It's definitely a growth. We'd have to operate in order to find out whether it's malignant or not. We have to treat it quickly, because she'll die if it gets into her lungs."

I was frozen to the spot, and it felt as if my legs

would give way. I turned to look for a chair. But Daniela was already sitting there, with tears pouring down her face. And when our eyes met, she sobbed out aloud. You didn't understand what was going on. You were only interested in the door which would allow us to get away from that place which smelled so bad, and which was making Daniela cry. When you noticed her crying, you tried to wriggle out of my arms towards her, as if to say: "She needs me, let me go." I placed you onto her lap, and you stood and licked away her tears. It was your way of saying: "Please don't cry. I'm here now, and I love you."

I watched you. You were just as beautiful and agile as ever, with your eyes shining brightly. How could you be suffering from something so terrible?

"Doctor, is she going to die?" I asked. As he watched Daniela, and heard my low, shaky voice, he possibly began to understand that we'd been dealt an enormous blow. Maybe he didn't really care, but his tone did seem to change. He told us not to worry, because the lungs weren't affected yet, and that this disease didn't have to be fatal, as long as we didn't waste any time. He was being a bit kinder, but what good was that? You were sick, even though we couldn't see it, even though you wagged your tail as you sniffed the grass verges on our way home, and hurried along because that doctor had made us late for your dinnertime. We walked, in silence, behind you. Daniela was crying. I kept quiet, and kicked myself for taking you to see the vet right there and then, as if any delay would have changed the truth of the matter.

It was Sunday the following day, and we took you to the vet in Milan on Monday. We were hoping that maybe the vet in Nizza had been wrong, but it was not to be. "We must operate immediately, tomorrow", he said.

Meanwhile, Isabella was due back from her summer holiday. She had 'phoned us a couple of evenings ago, and asked: "How's Kalé?" We'd told her that you were fine, just like always. Just forty eight hours later, everything had changed.

The next day, all three of us were sitting in the waiting room, ready for the nurse to come and give you your pre-op injection. Then they would take you inside, to make you better. It was difficult to believe, because you were so content, joyful, and full of life.

There were others in the waiting room too. I'll never forget the old man cradling his sick pet, which had tired, sad, hopeless eyes. He was stroking it, and murmuring: "I've got to let them do a third operation. The vet says there's no other way." He sighed, and tears rolled slowly down his cheeks onto his pet's fur. He said: "If they don't operate on you, you'll die. You may die even if they do operate. Your weak old heart's got to pull you through. You'll pull through if your heart makes it. You've only got to get through this, and then I think I'll be taking you home. The vet says that you might not make it even if you get through the operation. But we'll get you home first, and then we'll see how it goes."

The old man was clinging onto hope, but he said, distraughtly: "You're the only thing I've got. What'll I do if you die?"

Other people came with their pets, and those who'd brought hopeless cases to see the vet talked to their pets as they waited.

I realized as we waited there that we were not alone in loving you so much. But it's not true that pain brings people together, that it creates a bond. Deep within, each of us is just looking out for ourselves, and we keep hope alive for our own benefit. We can't allow other people's sadness to touch us, because our own hearts are already overflowing with bitterness and fear.

Then they came, took you away, and closed the door behind them. And the waiting began. You were carried in by a nurse, and your eyes searched us out as if to ask: "Why are you abandoning me? Why aren't you coming too?" The door opened again after an hour and a half, and you were returned to us with your eyes closed, your fur all ruffled and untidy. Your face had lost its wonderful expressiveness. Your white fur was stained with red where the wound had bled. Isabella said to me: "You take her, I can't bear to see her like this." And you were still asleep as we took you back home.

Isabella laid you down nearby so that she could watch over you as you slept. I went out, and she 'phoned me to tell me that you were still asleep, and hadn't moved. That evening, however, as you heard the church bell ringing, you could smell me as I approached the front door. No-one noticed as I came in and called out: "How is she?", but you got up and staggered over to me, wagging your tail in your usual greeting. Just not as quickly as usual. Your tail wagged slowly. Daniela said: "Poor little thing. She's not well. But she managed to get up to greet you." Isabella picked you up, and laid you down near her again. She was worried in case the wound opened up. The doctor had advised us to keep you still.

They were difficult, worrying days, but also encouraging. We could see you getting better as the hours went by. You were back to your old self after only a week had passed.

You were eating again, jumping up, talking, going out. We took you for a check up, and the vet told us: "It's fine. Everything's just fine. The danger's past."

And this is what he told us each month when we went for a regular check up. You'd recovered fully. The wound had stopped hurting, and you'd forgotten all about that terrible place where we'd taken you and made you suffer. And we'd forgotten, too. Our life was back to normal, and was running smoothly again. We'd got over the terror and fright which we'd felt.

One morning, however, six months later, Daniela called me as I was getting out of the shower. Her voice was subdued, but I could hear that she was alarmed: "Oh my God, I can feel that thing again." "What thing?" I asked, but I already knew what she meant. Fate had us in its sights, and it didn't want to let us get away. I felt you as well. The disease had returned, and in several places this time. Six months down the line, and we were back in that horrible place again. There were different people and different pets. We were the only things that were the same, with hearts full of anguish for a second time.

We'd already been through it all once, but that didn't make it any easier now. Your fur all stained with red again, the house all dark again so that you could rest, and then back to your old way of life once again. Everything went well the second time, too. We felt a bit calmer. We stroked you every day, down there where the disease had invaded you. There was no sign of it.

We went on holiday. We went back to Nizza, where we'd first discovered that you weren't well, exactly one year ago.

But we were relaxed this time. You were all right, and we'd put those awful thoughts behind us which had haunted our hearts and minds.

Our last three days of happiness

My greatest regret is not realizing that you were about to leave us. We were taking a three day vacation in Nizza, and you weren't very well. Your legs seemed to be hurting, you didn't want to go for walks. You'd always loved going out, and the fact that you didn't want to, pulling against the lead and planting your feet on the floor, meant that you were trying to tell us something. "Is it because the tarmac scorches your paws, because you have to go barefoot on these hot streets?" It really was extremely hot, and we thought that this was why you weren't on form.

You didn't jump about as much at home. You were quiet, and would still be lying around even when we got up in the morning. We called you and called you, and you'd eventually come downstairs, not because you wanted to, but just to please us. Your tail hardly wagged when you greeted us, just from side to side two or three times.

Daniela began to get worried. "I know Kalé", she said, "No-one knows her as well as I do. Something's wrong when she does that." As usual, she panicked if you didn't seem to be your usual self. I teased her:

"And to think you didn't want her at first. Now you watch every breath she takes. You're always worried, watching over her, even more than you did with Isabella when she was little."

No-one could fully comprehend the unique bond that had formed between you, not even me. You knew how to let her know what you were thinking, what you were saying, and how you were feeling, because she understood everything about you. She anticipated your movements, and could diagnose what was wrong with you even before the vet could. Her panic stemmed from the fact that she knew you so well, and her diagnosis was correct. Once again, she'd foreseen what was about to happen, because she knew that something wasn't quite right.

Whilst still on vacation, she telephoned the vet, and he tried to reassure her: "She doesn't want to go for walks because her back is hurting a bit. Is she still eating?" Daniela replied that she was. She was still eating with her usual appetite. "Well, if she's still eating, then there's no problem", the vet said. "You see, if there was anything seriously wrong, then the first sign would be lack of appetite."

She smiled as she put the receiver down. It wasn't a relieved smile, however, and she wasn't completely reassured. She repeated: "He says that her back's hurting a bit." Meanwhile, you lay stretched out on your belly, listening to her, and you heard the sadness in her voice. You realized that she, and only she, knew that you weren't well, and you didn't get up even when she said: "Come on, Kalé, let's go and get your food ready."

I tried not to take her fears seriously, preferring to believe what the vet said, as this was easier to accept, more reassuring.

You seemed to get better then. You started to move a bit quicker. We even decided to take you out. "I'll carry her", I said. We didn't leave you alone for a moment during those three days on vacation. You came to the department stores with us to choose some bedding for the new house, and I held you tight in my arms. Every now and again, I would have to shake off morbid thoughts, lowering my face towards your little head so that I could gently kiss your white fur.

I didn't like the fact that you didn't respond to me. It was the first time that you hadn't returned my kiss by giving me a lick. On the last night, we even took you to Montecarlo, to the restaurant where we were meeting up with some friends. I didn't make you lie down on the floor as usual, but kept you on my lap the whole time, perhaps because I had a premonition of what was to come, or maybe just because I was aware that your back was hurting. You buried your head under my napkin. I said: "Come on, come out from under there. They won't think anything of it here in Montecarlo, because they love little dogs like you." But you didn't feel up to it, you felt safe as you were. Hidden like this, you didn't care what happened as long as we kept you close to us. And just the feel of our bodies was enough for you. You didn't seem to need anything else. Afterwards, we headed for the underground car park, and we passed lots of beautiful parks with long grass. There were signs declaring that no dogs were allowed. However, I put you down, wondering if the fresh smell of the grass and flowers would invigorate you. I watched as you rushed about, wagging your tail and sniffing everywhere. You peed all over the place – a sign of how excited you were – and you looked at me as if to express your gratitude for allowing you to run free in such a wonderful place. It's the last memory I have of you being happy. This is how I want to remember you, and I concentrate on this memory when thoughts of you suddenly overwhelm me, when I think I just can't bear it because you're not here any more.

I imagine you in that park, your tail wagging vigorously, sniffing at the flowers in the grass, and watering them with three little drops of pee. You seemed full of life, a young pup again. I said to Daniela: "Look, she's back to her old self again. It's cooler this evening, and she feels all right. It really was the hot sun that was making her feel ill. See? She was all weak during the day, but you can see that she's just fine this evening."

As she watched you, she too convinced herself that this was the case. She watched you wagging your tail as you ran through the grass, and she was relieved.

"You know, I was just worried because I thought that Isabella wouldn't be able to bear it if something happened." She was lying. She *was* thinking of Isabella, but she was also thinking about herself, because she wouldn't have been able to bear it either if you were ill again. She panicked every time you coughed, turned pale every time you sneezed, and made a drama out of the fact that you weren't eating. "It's no good thinking about Isabella now," I said, "She's away on vacation."

She decided: "It makes me happy just seeing her like this", as she watched you peeing on a pretty red flower. She looked at you squatting over this flower, all hunched up, and you looked at her. She said: "Go on, give a few drops to that lovely flower."

You never usually peed in lots of little droplets. You normally did one long pee and got it over with. You only did it like this, with a few drops here, then a few drops there, when you were excited. It was Sunday, and I now wonder what we would have done that evening, what we would have said to you, how much we would have cuddled you, if we'd known that you'd no longer be with us in just a week's time, Kalé.

The following day, I left you at the airport. We went together in the taxi with Daniela. I talked to you as we travelled. You were lying on Daniela's stomach as usual. You were relaxed. You'd managed the stairs, you'd gone off to pee before getting in the taxi, and then you jumped right up onto the seat.

You appeared to be back on form, and I didn't have any worries as I left. I stroked your head and, when my hand stopped moving, you placed your paw on it. I commented to Daniela: "Look how cute she is, putting her paw out as if to stop me moving my hand away." And maybe you really did want to stop me going. I gave you a kiss before getting out of the taxi, and you looked at me with sad eyes.

"Come on, everything's all right now", I said as I kissed Daniela goodbye. She agreed: "Yes, I know, I can see she's better, I'm all right." You returned with her to our house in Liguria, but she still wasn't totally convinced. And so, the following day, she took you for a check up at the vet's. She rang me: "I took her along because I was still doubtful, but everything's all right. She's fine."

This was on Tuesday morning. On Wednesday morning, however, you were definitely not well. She noticed something was wrong straight away. She rang me around mid-day. She was in tears. "She's ill, she's ill. The vet just doesn't understand. She's bleeding inside." I said, "I'm leaving at once, and coming straight home." But the vet rang me, and said: "She's not in any danger, she's got over the worst. There's no need for you to come home. Come back on Friday just as you'd planned."

I was due to come back on Friday, when Isabella came home from vacation.

The telephone rang constantly during Wednesday

and Thursday. The vet said: "She's not in any danger. She's getting better."

Daniela, however, told me: "I don't think she's very well. She's so still. She never gets up, and she's not eating. She's not going to make it."

"What makes you say that? The vet says that she's getting better."

"No, I know her. She's ill, she's not eating or moving. She's listless. She looks at me so sadly, as if she's asking for help. She's dying, I think she's dying."

"Come on, don't say that. Isabella's coming home tomorrow, and she'll pick up then."

"No, she's hanging on for Isabella before she dies. She doesn't want to go without saying goodbye. I can sense it."

We got home the next day. We'd had a miserable journey, because I told Isabella that you weren't well, that Daniela was worried, and that we should get home as soon as possible. She immediately sensed that it was something serious.

"But the vet says she'll get better, so we have to believe him," I said.

But Isabella didn't take any notice, and cried. We got home, and saw you. You were stretched out, lying still, on the floor. You couldn't find the strength to get up and meet us. "It's getting worse," Daniela said. "Even the vet's worried today." You just lay there. Isabella knelt down by you, and your tail moved a little: you'd managed to summon up all your energy to greet her and let her know how pleased you were to see her. Then you stopped moving. She talked to you, stroked you, hugged you. You just lay still, looking at her woefully, your eyes distant, not following our movements at all.

We went to the vet's. Isabella and I took you. I drove. You were lying in her arms.

The vet started you on a drip, gave you an injection, and then more tests. Isabella was stroking you. She asked me to leave the room so that she could be alone with you. I could see her talking to you. When I came back, you were in a very bad way.

Isabella knew before I did. "She's going, she's going. You waited for me, Kalé. You wanted to wait for me. I loved you so much."

It was true, Kalé. You'd waited for her. You'd hung on because you didn't want to go without saying goodbye. So you slowly wagged your tail, and then stopped fighting, you couldn't do it any more.

Your breathing became fainter.

I asked the vet: "Is she in pain?"

"Yes."

"Isn't there anything we can do?"

"No", it was like you had been sentenced.

"Has she got long?"

"Not long."

I said: "Come on, Kalé, come on", as I held the oxygen mask close to your muzzle.

But you couldn't fight it, because you were no longer there. You couldn't hear me. Isabella stroked you for the last time, kissed you, and said: "I loved you very much."

Then she left. She wanted me to stay with you right until the end. She couldn't bear to see her Kalé like this any more.

It wasn't long, now. I took your muzzle between my hands. I lowered my head down close to your muzzle. I wanted you to be able to smell me. I hoped that you could sense that I was near you, and that we weren't leaving you.

I sensed that you were no longer there, even though your shallow breathing and heartbeat told me that there was still a link between us. I hugged you tighter, angry, thinking how unfair it was that you had to go. My tears fell onto you. I whispered: "Isabella's just over there. You heard her. She told you that she loved you very much." At that moment, your shallow breathing stopped, and I could no longer hear your irregular heartbeat. And it felt as if someone had taken you out of my arms, because I felt lighter, even though you were still there with me.

Kalé, I've been told since I was a child about a place to which, one by one, all the grown ups that I love will go. I can't even begin to imagine what it's like, but I used to think that it must be a horrible place if it takes away all the people whom we love. I've tried, but I've never been able to picture it in my mind. I can see it now, Kalé. You helped me see it at that moment when, whilst holding you close, I could no longer hear your breathing. I told you that it felt as if someone came and took you out of my arms. I know that's true now. Somebody did come and take you out of my arms, so that they could hold you close.

It wasn't just my imagination; it was Jesus, and this gives me comfort as I think about your final moments. You helped me believe that Jesus took pity on you at that moment, and took pity on us in our grief, and decided to take you from my arms and to hold you close to Him.

I actually saw you. You suddenly became radiant. Your fur was no longer all messed up, but became sleek and shiny. All signs of pain and suffering left your face. You were already far away.

I was not ashamed of crying in front of the vet. I wrapped you up in the blanket we'd laid you in when we left the house.

I left the room holding you in my arms, and saw the grief in Isabella's eyes.

We took you to a friend's garden that very evening. We dug a hole, arranged the blanket around you, and laid you in a box. The box was lowered into the ground and covered with earth. The following day, Isabella planted a rose-bush right there, on your grave.

But it wasn't over. We saw you everywhere we

went. Isabella asked me if pets had souls, too. "If they do," she said, "then she's still here."

I could only reply with another question: "No-one's ever convinced me that men have souls, just as no-one's ever convinced me that pets have souls, either. If men have souls, then why shouldn't wonderful little creatures like you have them, too?"

And so I became convinced that, at the moment of death, the Lord came and took away your soul, and just left your body with me.

I'm convinced that this is so, because I can now picture that place, for the first time ever.

And it's not a bad place. I can see food, I can see my grandparents, I can see Anna. And I can also see you, Kalé, running about wagging your tail, sniffing amongst the grass and flowers. You can't hear any of the traffic noise which you disliked so much, or smell any of the traffic fumes which used to bother you when we let you out to do your business first thing in the morning.

We never knew, Kalé, what took you away from us – what had taken place during those three days. We hadn't felt the need to ask whether the disease which had already caused to you undergo two operations had suddenly broken out again. We hadn't wanted to inquire whether something else had happened, something which nobody understood. We hadn't wanted to ask whether there'd been a mistake made in the attempts to treat you. We hadn't felt like questioning why you'd been snatched away from us just when we'd stopped fearing for your safety, and we were happy because it looked as if you were finally cured.

We hadn't questioned anything. We'd started to lose you a year before, that morning when we were at the airport, on vacation, and we felt the small lump next to one of your teats for the first time. And you can't give us any answers from that place where you are now.

But you're there. I know that now.

Loving means suffering too

Time passed quickly, and we hadn't realized that time went by quicker for you, Kalé, than for us.

It had been wonderful, even if it had gone by so quickly, and you taught us so many things.

Kalé, you taught us that love has no limits. You taught us that when you open up your heart, you can never have enough. You taught us that as soon as you think you're no longer vulnerable, your armour is suddenly stripped off. You taught us that as soon as you think you're comfortably settled at the station of life, another train comes along unexpectedly, you get on, and encounter someone just like you.

You were just a ball of white fluff, but you gradually made yourself at home with us, won us over, and showed us a new way of life. I've learnt that there's room in my heart for more than just my partner and my daughter. I've realized that there's room for others, and not just friends and family. I know now that even a little dog can have the key to my heart, and is able to enter in it and never leave.

I loved you, Kalé, and I still love you now. But loving means suffering too. Yesterday, as she stood near that piece of ground where your body now lies, Daniela sobbed uncontrollably. She said: "Even if I live another hundred years, I'll never get over this." It's just like that: we'll never get over it. But it's only through grief that we can remember you, the sweet torment that suddenly brings you back, as our eyes fill with tears. This is the power of love.

If someone were to say to me: "I can take away the grief, get rid of your heartache with a single wave of my magic wand, but it would mean erasing all your memories of her as well, as if you'd never known her, as if you'd never seen her", I wouldn't let them do it. I'd rather suffer, and never forget you. Kalé, you taught me that even this suffering is what life is all about. You lie under that piece of ground, but my heart still burns for you. I look at the place where you're buried. I imagine you, lying there, covered in white fur, and wrapped in the blanket in which I so carefully laid you. I see that you're sleeping. I can't think of you in any other way. I can see how upset Daniela is, how Isabella strokes the earth, blows you a kiss, and tends to the roses with which she has surrounded you. I tell myself that you loved them more than you loved me, and that their love for you was greater than mine. But, as I feel how heavy my heart is, I ask myself: can we really measure love? You also taught us this, Kalé: love has no limits. If there are limits, then that's not really love. And even if you're down there and we're here looking at a piece of earth surrounded by roses, the love which began that day in the shop when you licked me for the first time, is still not over because I sense that you're there in that place which you, and only you, helped me to see. Not even death can destroy the life that we had together: Daniela, Isabella, me, and you, my love.

Kalé, I've written about, and relived, our story – not as an outlet for my grief, or even to tell others about our life together. No, I've written it all down because, if there's one thing I've always been able to do, it's to use a pen, writing down all the things which I feel inside. And so I've put our story into writing. Time flies by so quickly, and it took you away so soon. If it takes my memory along with it, I'll always have these words to remind me of you.

Words which I'll always be able to read, even if the memories fade.

Words which I've decided to publish, because everyone should know what a little creature like you can do. A small dog which looked just like a white ball of fluff.

Many would think it impossible, but it was you, only you, who helped me discover that I know how to believe.

Thank you for filling our hearts with love, Kalé.

Index

We kissed when we first met 7

Your name means "pretty" in Greek 17

The lambswool coat incident 19

We begin to communicate 25

Only nice words 29

More than just a gift 37

Our wonderful times at Christmas 43

An evening of Shakespeare at the theater 47

You slept beside me 53

I even took you to the office 57

Fate was about to take an interest in our happiness 63

Our last three days of happiness 75

Loving means suffering too 87

Stefano Masi and Enrico Lancia
ITALIAN MOVIE GODDESSES
Over 80 of the Greatest Women of Italian Cinema
226 pages • US$ 29.95/£ 19.95

Jean A. Gili
ITALIAN FILMMAKERS
Self Portraits: A Selection of Interviews
192 pages • US$ 24.95/£ 15.95

ITALIAN DANCE AND OPERA

Roberta Albano, Nadia Scafidi and Rita Zambon
DANCE IN ITALY
From the 18th Century to the Present Day
La Scala of Milan – San Carlo of Naples – La Fenice of Venice
192 pages • US$ 32.50/£ 19.95

Enrico Stinchelli
GREATES STARS OF THE OPERA
The Lives and Voices of Two Hundred Golden Years
224 pages • US$ 32.50/£ 19.95

COOKING ITALIAN WAY

Maria Chiara Martinelli
AL DENTE
All the Secrets of Italy's Genuine Home-Style Cooking
208 pages • US$ 29.95/£ 18.95 (P/b US$ 19.95/£ 12.95)

Paolo Scotto
WINE AND CHEESE OF ITALY
160 pages • US$ 29.95/£ 14.95